The Boy Who Made An Elephant

Stig Andersson

© Bokforlaget Libris, Orebro, Sweden
Printed in England 1979
by Purnell & Sons Ltd, Paulton (Bristol) and London
Coedition arranged with the help of Angus Hudson, London
ISBN 91-7194-169-X

American Edition
Chariot Books
David C. Cook Publishing Company
Elgin, IL 60120
ISBN 0-89191-190-1

It was raining, and Peter sat inside looking out the window. He wondered what to do.

His sister Lisa was in school, and none of his friends were allowed out in the rain.

If he only had a pet to play with. But what kind of pet?

There were already enough dogs in the neighborhood. And besides, the neighbor's dogs barked, and weren't at all friendly.

Peter wanted to have a pet that was different from everybody else's.

Why not a bird? "A stork with long red legs might not be so dumb. Maybe I could even fly on its back?"

But, no, not a stork.

A tall, tall giraffe would be much more practical. Peter could climb up its neck, and fetch all the balls he had lost in the house's rain gutter.

But what would he do with a giraffe at night?

A little animal then? A ladybug. But ladybugs fly away as soon as you breathe in their direction.

Peter had once seen a picture of a toucan. What a beak that bird had! But with such a big beak, a toucan would probably bite. Ouch!

A rhinoceros maybe? No, they look like monsters made of steel, and are probably dangerous with that big horn they have on their noses.

"Now I know what I want . . .

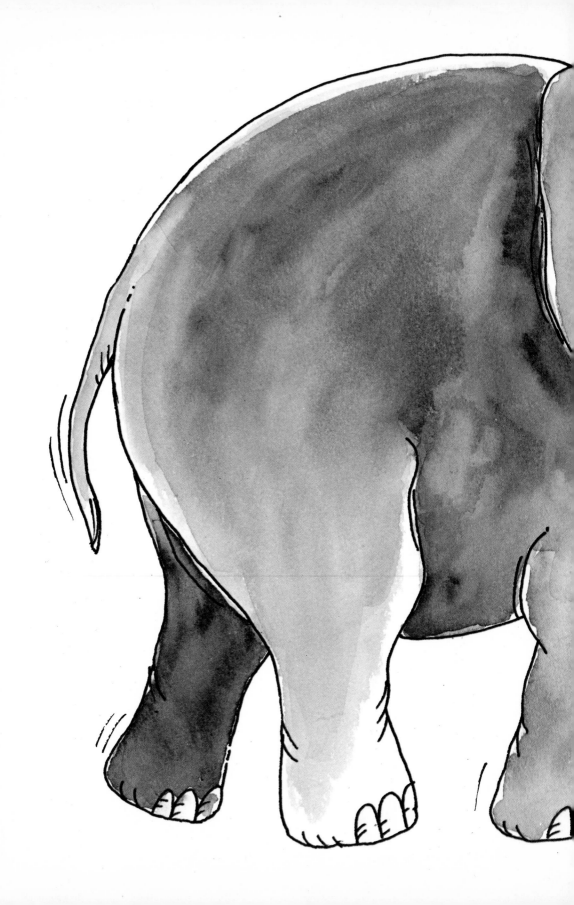

an elephant! An elephant
would make a perfect pet."
    Peter had seen elephants
both at the circus and on TV.
    They were so much fun. As
big as a house, with ears that
flapped like wings. And a long
funny nose called a trunk.

Elephants are proud of their trunks. They can pick fruit from trees and grass from the ground with their trunks.

They can fill their trunks with water and squirt it out again like a fireman with a fire hose.

Elephants can blow their trunks like a horn, too, sounding like a brass band.

And elephants are strong.

The people in India sometimes use elephants instead of tractors. Peter would plow with his elephant, too.

He would sit high up on his elephant's back, and ride him wherever he wanted to go.

They would pull tree trunks out of the woods and build a log cabin where Peter and the elephant could live together.

When they weren't busy building their house, they would perform difficult tricks. Just like the circus.

Or maybe Peter would arrange a concert featuring the world's largest trumpet. . . .

Of course, he couldn't be sure that anyone would come and listen.

When we get hot and sweaty, we'll find a lake somewhere, thought Peter. *When you're friends with an elephant, you always have a shower with you.*

Peter wondered where he could buy an elephant. He had never seen an elephant at the pet store, or a sign saying FRESH ELEPHANTS ON SALE TODAY, either.

But maybe he could make one himself.
I'll give it a try, he decided.

He had always thought that elephants looked like they were made from clay.

And he had plenty of clay at home. He could start immediately.

He began by rolling a big lump of clay into a ball.
That was the elephant's body. A smaller lump
became the elephant's head.

 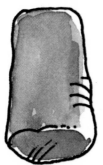  

An elephant's legs look like big, thick logs. They
were easy to roll out.

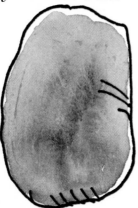 

He made the ears by flattening out two small balls
of clay. Just like that!

Peter rolled out a beautiful trunk. He was extra careful with it. Finally, he made a little tail, and fetched two buttons for eyes.

He now had all the parts. It didn't take long to put the elephant together. And it *was* a fine elephant!

I can make elephants, thought Peter proudly. *Now let's see what he can do with his trunk.*

"I wish I had a little grass he could eat, or a little water for him to squirt.

"Well, he can at least play the trumpet!"

Peter stretched out the trunk a little, and shaped it into a trumpet to make the job easier for the elephant.

"Okay, do your stuff," said Peter. "Play a tune for me. Play something. Anything! Please . . . nice Mr. Elephant. . . ."

Nothing happened.

I must have done something wrong, thought
Peter.

"If I make his trunk look like a bugle
instead, then I bet he can play."

And so he made a fine-looking bugle out of
the elephant's trunk.

"Okay, let's hear it! . . .

"*Let's hear it! . . .*

"*L E T'S   H E A R   I T!*"

The elephant didn't make a sound.

"Never mind! It doesn't matter!" and he threw the elephant to the floor.

"What was that?" asked Lisa, who had just come home from school.

"My elephant," sobbed Peter.

"Did you make an elephant?"

"Yes, but it wasn't so fine. It couldn't blow its horn, I mean trunk. It couldn't do ANYTHING."

"But, Peter, you know that you can't make a clay elephant that can use its trunk like a trumpet, or squirt out water, or do any of those things that a real elephant can do."

"An elephant is a complicated creature," Lisa went on.

"An elephant has a brain, just like you, so it can decide by itself when it wants to blow its trumpet.

"His big stomach needs food, so he can walk, grow, or do any of the things a real elephant does.

"And it has a heart, just like yours, which keeps him alive.

"God created all these things. And without them an elephant can't live. Only God can create life."

"But Peter, we, too, can be creative." said
Lisa. "We can draw pictures of elephants.
Funny pictures.

"Go get some paper and crayons, and let's
see if we can draw some elephants together."

So Peter drew checkered elephants. And polka dot elephants.

And Lisa drew a whole family with funny clothes!

But the elephants were not alive. They stayed on the papers where they were drawn.

It's just as well that only God can make real elephants.

Otherwise a boy like Peter might create pink elephants who flew around houses and blew their trumpets in the middle of the night when everyone wanted to sleep.